Edgar Badger's
Fishing
Day

Edgar Badger's Fishing Day

by Monica Kulling

illustrated by Neecy Twinem

MONDO

For my brother Edwin, with love—M.K.

To Augie and Sylvia, with love—N.T.

Text copyright © 1999 by Monica Kulling
Illustrations copyright © 1999 by Neecy Twinem

For information contact:
MONDO Publishing
980 Avenue of the Americas,
New York, NY 10018

Visit our web site at http://www.mondopub.com

Designed by Eliza Green
Production by The Kids at Our House

Printed in Hong Kong
01 02 03 04 05 06   9 8 7 6 5 4 3 2

Library of Congress Cataloging-in-Publication Data

Kulling, Monica.
     Edgar Badger's fishing day / by Monica Kulling ; illustrated
by Neecy Twinem.
          p.   cm.
     Summary: Edgar Badger and his best friend Duncan Bear
have a squabble when they go on a fishing trip.
     ISBN 1-57255-603-X (alk. paper)
     [1. Badgers—Fiction. 2. Bears—Fiction. 3. Fishing—
Fiction. 4. Best friends—Fiction. 5. Friendship—Fiction.]
I. Twinem, Neecy, ill. II. Title.
PZ7.K9490155Ec   1999
[E]—dc21   97-32039
                                                               CIP
                                                               AC

Contents

Gone Fishing

*T*he sun was just rising and Edgar Badger was ready for a day of fishing. His favorite hat was on his head. His grub salad sandwiches were packed. His fishing box and pole were by the door.

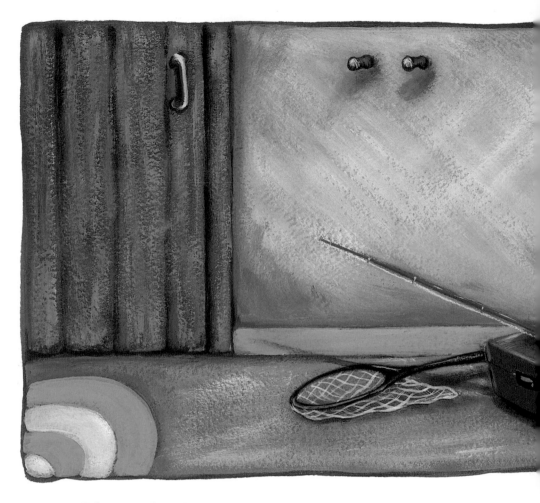

The only thing missing was his
neighbor, Duncan Bear. Edgar sat
down to wait. He sat and wondered.
*Can Duncan and I get along for one
whole day without fighting?*

"After we went hang-gliding, we didn't
speak to each other for a week," sighed
Edgar. "But maybe fishing will be
different. We've never tried fishing."

9

Suddenly there was a knock at the door. Edgar waddled over to open it. There stood Duncan in a funny fishing hat.

"Funny hat," said Duncan. "But my hat is funnier. And it keeps out the sun better."

He's starting already, thought Edgar.

Edgar picked up his fishing box and pole. He closed his front door and put up a sign.

Renting a Boat

*E*dgar and Duncan had their first squabble at Sally Otter's marina. "Do you have a roomy rowboat for rent?" Edgar asked Sally.

"What do you mean, a rowboat?" asked
Duncan.

"A rowboat would be best," said Edgar.
"We don't want to make any noise. We
want to sneak up on the fish."

"Sneak up?" replied Duncan. "How can we sneak up if it takes all day to get to the fish? Fish bite in the early morning, you know. We need speed!"

"The Turbo Monster is my fastest
boat," said Sally. "It will get you
across the lake in a wink."
"That's perfect!" exclaimed Duncan.
He hopped into the speedboat.

Edgar sighed and climbed into the
speedboat, too. He sat down. He put
his fishing box and pole at his feet.
"Have you ever worked one of these
before?" Edgar asked nervously.
"No," replied Duncan. "But it's easy.
See this cord? You just pull it . . ."

Duncan pulled the cord with all his
might. The motor roared to life.
". . . and we're off!" he yelled.

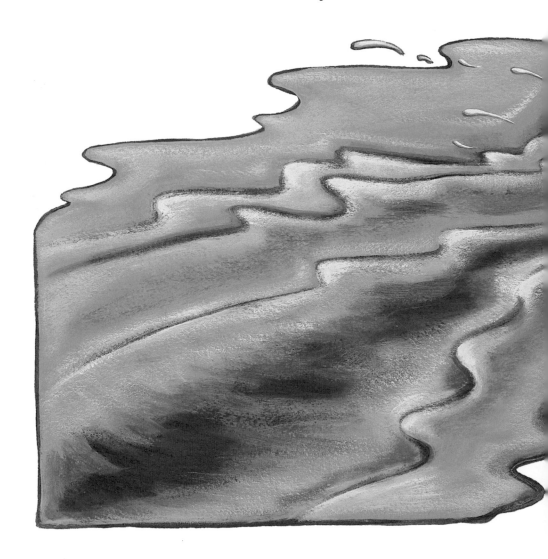

The Turbo Monster shot across
Pine Lake. It cut deep white waves
behind it.

Edgar hung onto his fishing pole. He hung onto his fishing box. But most of all, he hung onto his favorite hat.

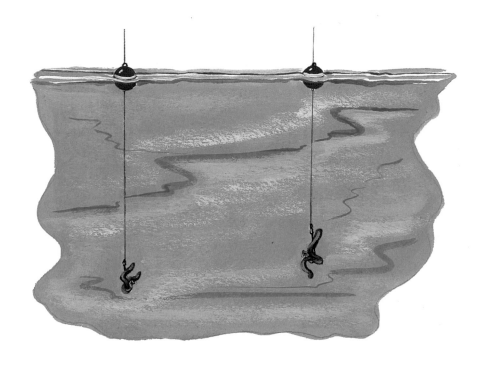

Waiting

The boat was resting calmly in the middle of the lake. Edgar had a worm on his fishing line. Duncan had a worm on his fishing line. Both lines were in the water.

Edgar and Duncan waited. And waited. And waited some more.

"I love the mist on the lake in the early morning," said Edgar.

"Me too," said Duncan. But he wasn't really listening.

"Did I tell you my sister Isabelle is coming for dinner tonight?" asked Edgar. "I hope I catch a fish. Isabelle is very fond of fish."

"Me too!" replied Duncan. This time
he *was* listening. He smacked his lips,
thinking of dinner.

Suddenly there was a tug on Edgar's line. This was it! Isabelle would have a fine fish for dinner.

A Big Fish

*T*here was a BIG fish on Edgar's line.
Edgar pulled with all his might.
"Give me the pole," said Duncan,
grabbing for it. "I'm bigger. I'm stronger.
I can land this fish in a flash."

"I can land my own fish," said Edgar. He pulled his pole away from Duncan's grabbing paws.

Edgar fought with the fish. The fish fought with Edgar.

"I'm bigger and stronger," Duncan repeated. He grabbed for Edgar's pole again. The boat rocked wildly.

"So what?" said Edgar. "This is *my* fish."

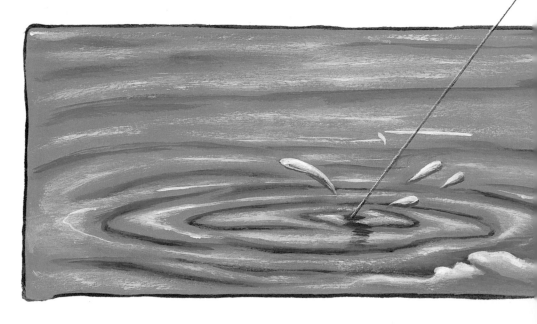

Edgar fought for the pole. Duncan
fought for the pole. Suddenly the pole
flew out of their paws. It flew and the
fish got away.

Edgar slumped down in the boat. "There goes Isabelle's fish," he sighed. "I could have pulled it in," mumbled Duncan. "You should have let me help you."

At dinner that night, Isabelle looked
at her plate of earwigs and beetles.

"I had my taste buds all set for a fine
fish," she said, disappointed.

Edgar sighed. Now he felt even worse about the fish. And it was all Duncan's fault.

Friends Again

*T*wo weeks went by. Isabelle came for dinner again. Amanda Salamander and Violet Porcupine were invited, too.

Edgar served a bowl of worms and acorns. He also served grubs and greens and a side dish of snails.

"What a feast," said Isabelle. "This is as fine as fish."

"I'll take your word for it," said Violet. She looked at the worms on her plate.

"I've never tried snails," remarked Amanda.

"You'll love them," said Isabelle. "But they're not quite as tasty as fish. And speaking of fish, how is Duncan?" she asked Edgar.

"I don't know," replied Edgar. He twirled a worm on his fork. "We haven't spoken since the day my fish got away."

"That's a long time for friends not to speak to each other," said Isabelle.

"And you and Duncan are *best*
friends," added Violet.

Amanda just nodded. She was busy
trying to swallow her first snail.

"Some friend," mumbled Edgar. "He's always pushing his weight around." Isabelle cut into a worm. She didn't want to badger Edgar, but she had to have her say.

"You know, Duncan may turn out to
be the friend that got away," she said
gently.

After everyone left, Edgar thought
about Isabelle's words.

Early the next morning, Edgar
knew what he had to do. He walked
out his front door and headed for
Duncan's house.

But who should be coming up the path to Edgar's house? Duncan! And he was carrying the biggest fish Edgar had ever seen.

"I had a visitor last night," Duncan mumbled. "She said you'd like a fine fish."

Duncan handed Edgar the fish. Edgar could hardly stand under its great weight.

"You *are* a strong bear," said Edgar. "Let's have fish for breakfast."

"It's never too early for a fine feast of fish," Duncan agreed.